This Little Tiger book belongs to:

_____

_____

_____

_____

For Isobel and Tom ~ D B
For all the little bears in my world ~ C P

LITTLE TIGER PRESS

1 The Coda Centre, 189 Munster Road, London SW6 6AW
www.littletiger.co.uk

First published in Great Britain 2007
This edition published 2008

Text copyright © David Bedford 2007
Illustrations copyright © Caroline Pedler 2007
David Bedford and Caroline Pedler have asserted their rights to
be identified as the author and illustrator of this work under the
Copyright, Designs and Patents Act, 1988

Printed in China • LTP/3100/1567/0616

4 6 8 10 9 7 5 3

Bedtime
for Little Bears!

David Bedford   Caroline Pedler

LITTLE TIGER PRESS
London

Little Bear and his mother
had spent a long, sunny
day exploring in the snow.

"It's getting late," said Mother
Bear. "It will soon be bedtime.
Let's go home, Little Bear."

Little Bear flumped down in the snow and wiggled his tail. "I'm not sleepy," he said, "and I don't want to go to bed yet."

Mother Bear smiled. "Shall we have one last explore," she said, "and see who else is going to bed?"

Little Bear looked about. "Who else *is* going to bed?" he wondered.

Mother Bear stretched up tall to find out.

"Look there," she said.

"It's Little Owl!" said Little Bear.

"Little Owl likes to stretch her wings before bedtime, and feel the whisper of the soft night breeze in her feathers," said Mother Bear.

Little Bear scrambled on to his mother's shoulders.

"I like flying too!" he said.

As Mother Bear climbed to the top of a hill, Little Bear felt the wind whispering and tickling through his fur.

Then he saw someone else . . .

"Who's that?" said Little Bear, giggling.
"And what's he doing?"

"Baby Hare is having a bath in the
snow," said Mother Bear, "so that he's
clean and drowsy, and ready for sleep."

"I like snow baths too," said Little Bear. He dived into the snow and scattered it about, plopping a big, soft snowball on Mother Bear's nose.

Little Bear and his mother laughed as they flopped down together in a heap.

"Are you sleepy now, Little
Bear?" his mother asked as
they lay together in the snow,
watching the first bright stars
twinkling in the sky.

Little Bear blinked his tired eyes as he tried not to yawn. "I want to see who else is going to bed," he said.

"We'll have to be quiet now," said Mother Bear. "Some little ones will already be asleep."

"Look over there," whispered Mother Bear. "Little
Fox likes being cuddled and snuggled to sleep by
his mother."

Little Bear pressed close against Mother Bear's
warm fur. "I like cuddles too," he said.

"We'll be home soon," said his mother softly.

But Little Bear had just seen somebody else . . .

"I can see whales!" he said, turning to look out across the starlit sea.

"Little Whale likes his mother to sing him softly to sleep," said Mother Bear.

Little Bear sat with his mother and watched the whales swimming by until they were gone, leaving only the soothing hum of their far-away song. Then he yawned. "Are we nearly home yet?" he said drowsily.

Little Bear climbed on to his mother's back, and as he was carried home he watched the colours that flickered and brushed across the sky, while his mother sang him a lullaby.

"I like songs too," he told his mother.

"And now," said Mother Bear very softly, "it's time for little bears to go to sleep."

Little Bear nestled into his mother's soft fur, and when she gave him a gentle kiss goodnight . . .

. . . Little Bear was
already fast asleep.